A DECISION IS YOURS BOOK

on the
Bus

by Carl W. Bosch

$\frac{\begin{array}{r} 2 \\ +2 \end{array}}{4}$

Parenting Press
Inc.

illustrated by
Rebekah Strecker

LC 88-42650
ISBN 978-0-943990-42-2 paperback

Parenting Press
814 North Franklin Street
Chicago, Illinois 60610
www.ParentingPress.com

BEFORE YOU BEGIN

Most books you read tell you about other people's decisions.

This book is different! *You* make the decisions. *You* decide what happens next.

Have you ever made a decision and found things didn't turn out the way you planned? It happens all the time. Did you ever dream about going back and trying again? What would have happened if you had done something differently?

In this book you'll find out how it feels when a bully picks on you. You'll have lots of chances to choose different ways of acting. You make the decisions. Good luck!

Turn the page and see what happens.

You wait at the bus stop and chew on the end of **1**
your glove. A few flakes of snow begin to fall
lightly from the gray sky. You are hoping for a big
snow storm and a day off from school, but you're
out of luck.

Nick Jones is waiting for you on the bus. He is
the biggest, meanest kid in the fifth grade. You
had an argument with him last week. You like
one pro football team and Nick likes another. You
gave a lot of good reasons why you think your
team is better, but Nick called you a jerk. Now he
wants to settle the argument with a fight. He
picks on you every time he sees you. He said he
was going to punch your face in today.

You don't like to fight, but you don't want the
other kids to think you're a coward either. You're
not sure what to do.

Just then, Bus #42 comes around the corner. It
stops and the door swings open. You wait for a
minute and grab your book bag.

Mrs. Geller, the bus driver, calls out to you.

"Well, Jack, are you going to school today or
not?"

If you decide to get on the bus, turn to page 3.

If you decide not to get on the bus, turn to page 14.

You move down the middle of the bus and see that there are only a couple of seats left near the back. There is a rule against standing on the bus, so you move toward the back. You drop into one of the seats. In the seat beside you is your friend Ben. The bus starts off.

Softly at first and then getting louder, a voice comes from a couple of rows back.

"Oh Jackie? Jackie, Jackie, Jack-e-e," the voice rings out.

You know it's Nick. A few of his friends are laughing with him.

"Today's the day, Jackie-boy! Today's the day!"

More laughter comes from the back. Then a rubber band hits you in the back of the head. You are upset and worried and nervous all at the same time.

If you decide to move to a different seat, turn to page 9.

If you decide to stay in your same seat, turn to page 5.

"I'm not going to move," you whisper to Ben. "I'm not going to let that bully push me around."

"Okay," says Ben, "I'll stick with you."

Ben's words are hopeful, but his eyes look kind of worried. You don't know if it is the right idea to stay in your seat, but you're going to try. Another rubber band zooms by your head and hits the back of the seat in front of you.

"Who are you whispering to Jackie? Your girl friend?" Another round of laughter comes from the back of the bus.

The bus is only about half way to school and you don't think the teasing is going to stop. Then a broken pencil hits you in the back. You turn to look at Ben.

If you decide to ask Ben for help, turn to page 7.

If you decide to jump up and fight Nick, turn to page 11.

6

"Ben, I need some help and I need it fast. What do you think I should do?" you ask.

"Well, what have you thought of?" Ben asks.

"Not much yet, that's why I'm asking you."

Ben starts to offer you his ideas. "You could turn around and shoot a rubber band back at him, or yell at him. Sometimes that works. Of course, you can always go back there and pop him right in the nose. That would surprise him. Then you can sell me your BMX racer and move to Texas."

"Ben, I'm not joking," you respond. Another broken pencil whizzes past your head.

"I know. But Jack, most bullies are a lot of hot air and not much else. If you fight him it might show that he's just a lot of talk. On the other hand, you could just keep ignoring him."

"Ignore him?!" you answer.

"Sure," Ben replies, "my dad says that if you don't pay any attention to a bully, he'll get tired of all the fuss pretty quick."

You decide to ignore Nick.
Turn to page 20.

You decide to move to a different seat. There aren't a lot of seats open, but you see one about three rows up.

You jump up quickly and rush to the empty seat. Mrs. Geller looks back and tells you to sit down.

A loud burst of laughter from the back follows you. Everything is okay for about four minutes. Then, as the next group of kids gets on the bus, you notice that Nick has moved up also.

A minute later a broken pencil hits the back of your neck. Then another piece hits you in the head. More laughs come from the back.

You think, "I can't take this anymore."

You decide to ask the bus driver for help.
Turn to page 47.

If you decide to turn around and fight Nick,
turn to page 11.

You stand up and take your book bag with you. **11**
While Nick is looking at his friends you swing
your book bag at him. Nick ducks just in time and
the bag hits the back of the seat. He jumps up and
tries to punch you, but the space is too small.
You're quick and Nick is kind of slow. The kids on
the bus scream and yell.

You decide that the best way not to get hurt is to
wrestle. You grab Nick around the arms. This up-
sets your balance and you both fall over into the
aisle. The brakes on the bus screech to a halt.

Suddenly you hear Mrs. Geller's voice—and it's
a voice everybody listens to.

"Stop it! Stop this right now!"

Turn to page 50.

That night your mom tells you there are lots of ways to ignore teasing and keep calm when someone is picking on you.

"You can just close your ears and think of someplace that is fun—like the beach," she says.

"Or, you could imagine yourself surrounded by a special energy field. Then when Nick calls you names, those words just hit the special shield and turn into rain.

"Another idea is to breathe deeply. It sounds funny, but that helps."

You decide to take your mom's advice and try ignoring Nick. For a whole week you breathe deeply, think about the beach and sometimes imagine your energy field. After a while, Nick stops picking on you.

Every so often he comes out with a wise comment or yells something from across the playground. You ignore him, not even turning around to look. You can tell that his heart isn't really in it.

Maybe he teases someone else, but you don't know for sure. All you know is that he leaves you alone. You don't become friends, but that is okay.

The End

14   You decide you just can't get on that bus. You say, "No, Mrs. Geller, I forgot something at home, I'll get my mom to drive me."

"Jack, I'll have to tell them at school," she warns.

"That's okay. No problem. I'll probably beat you there."

The bus starts up, and then slows down again. Off jumps Ben Woods, your best friend. He runs over and says that he wants to help you out with the "Nick problem." As the bus moves on, you can hear Nick and his friends shouting from the back window.

"Don't they ever quit?" you ask.

"Yeah, Jack, they will, it just takes time."

"Maybe, but will I last that long?"

"Well, what do you want to do? Walk to school or ask your mom for a ride? If we walk, we'll be late. If we ask your mom, she'll want to know why we missed the bus," Ben points out.

If you decide to walk to school, turn to page 27.

If you decide to ask your mom for a ride, turn to page 17.

You go back to your house, walk inside, and yell to your mom, "We missed the bus. Can you take us to school?"

"We?" calls your mom from the study.

"Ben's here too," you call back.

"Is something wrong?" your mom asks.

"No," you answer quickly.

"Nick Jones," Ben answers at the same time. You give him a look like you want to turn him to stone.

"Nick Jones? What's going on?" your mom asks.

"He just wants to send me to the emergency room," you answer.

"Well, hop in the car and tell me about it on the way to school," your mom says. You knew you'd have to go to school, but at least you don't have to ride the bus.

On the way your mom tells you to stay out of Nick's way today. She says she will help you with some ideas when you get home tonight.

You nod your head and say "yes." Then you think that it's hard to ignore someone who throws mashed potatoes at you in the lunch room.

You arrive early at school. Your mom says, "I think you should talk to Ms. Wilkins about this too."

You say goodbye and jump out of the car.

If you decide to avoid Nick and wait to talk with your mom, turn to page 19.

If you decide to talk to Ms. Wilkins about it, turn to page 22.

After your mom drops you off, you walk down the hall with Ben trying to decide how to stay out of Nick's way. It's not an easy problem and it worries you all the time.

As you walk toward your classroom, you see through the windows that Bus #42 has rolled in.

You and Ben decide to go down to the bathroom. When you come out you see a few students in the hallway. About half way down the hall you see Nick. He really isn't doing anything, just standing and waiting for something to happen.

You decide to avoid him for the rest of the day.

Turn to page 12.

20 You decide to ignore Nick completely. All that day and the next, you don't even look at him. When you see him coming down the hall, you duck into a classroom, or make a detour. You never say a word back to him. On the bus, you ask Mrs. Geller if it would be all right to sit in the very first row.

Then comes the weekend. Since you won't see Nick for two days, you don't think about him.

Monday morning when you go down to the bus stop, your heart starts to beat a little faster. When Bus #42 swings around the corner you get on and hope for the best.

You don't look back, but you can hear Nick's voice above the others. He doesn't call out your name. In fact, he doesn't say a word to you—not that day, or the next.

Now when Bus #42 pulls around the corner in the morning, you have a big smile on your face.

The End

22 You knock on Ms. Wilkins' door. She is busy writing on the board.

"Jack and Ben," she says, "come on in. You're pretty early today."

"Ms. Wilkins, we... er... I... really need to talk to you. Nick Jones is driving me nuts. He wants to beat me up."

"Uh oh... sounds serious. Tell me the whole story," she says.

You tell her about how you and Nick just don't get along and about the argument over which pro football team is best. You tell her you tried to explain your side with logic, but Nick wanted to settle it with his fists.

"I think I understand. I can see two ways that you might handle this. First, I think you have to do more than just ignore him. You really have to work hard. Don't look at him in the hallway or on the bus. And make sure you don't say anything back to him. That should do the trick.

"The second idea is that I could call him in for a talk. You, me, and Nick. What do you think?"

If you decide to ignore Nick, turn to page 20.

If you decide to talk with him and Ms. Wilkins, turn to page 43.

Neither of you want to go see the principal and would rather solve it yourselves. You look at Nick and ask him if he wants to keep bugging you.

"It's kind of fun," he answers.

"Nick," Mrs. Geller jumps in, "if that's the case, then I'm taking you to the principal right now. Come on, let's go."

"No! No, I was only joking. I don't want to go to the principal. He'll call my parents and that is something I don't need. Look, I won't bug him if he just stays out of my way."

"That's fine by me," you say.

"If you keep your bargain—fine," says Mrs. Geller. "But there are no second chances. If you don't, I will send both of you to the principal."

Ben is waiting for you to get off the bus and immediately asks, "What happened?"

You tell him that you both decided to settle it and "that was that."

Now Nick doesn't bother you any more. He never shoots things at you in the cafeteria or on the bus. One day you notice that he has a new victim; someone in his own grade. You feel sorry for the kid, and you hope that he can solve his problem quickly. You are really glad that you solved *your* problem.

The End

On the way to school you and Ben have a good **27** talk.

"I know what it's like to get picked on," Ben says, "my brother does it to me all the time. And, once in the third grade a big kid in the fourth grade pushed me around for a while. All I did was ignore him. I know that sounds a lot easier than it really is, but it can work if you stick to it."

The idea sounds good. Of course, Ben is your best friend and usually has good advice, but you don't think this "ignoring plan" will work with Nick. "But, what *will* work?" you think.

Your dad says that the only thing bullies understand is force.

You think, "I don't really want to fight Nick—that seems crazy—but I might be able to stand up to him in some way."

Just as you come around the corner to school, Ben shouts, "Wait a minute! I have another idea! Something we can all do together."

If you decide to stand up to Nick, turn to page 39.

If you decide to hear Ben's new idea, turn to page 57.

You decide to go to the office. You are sick of **29**
Nick and you want him to stop bugging you. You
are also a little afraid that if you don't stop him
now, Nick will find something worse to do to you.

Mrs. Geller says "Okay, that's fine with me,
let's go."

You feel pretty embarrassed walking into
school with Nick and Mrs. Geller. You have to
wait fifteen minutes while she makes arrange-
ments to have your parents called. The entire time
Nick doesn't say a word, he just has a very angry
look on his face. You are angry too—and also a
little bit scared.

A little while later your mom comes into the office. She looks concerned. As you leave, you look
at Nick. He knows his parents are on their way—
and now he looks nervous.

The End

Mrs. Geller takes both of you to the principal's office. Before you know it, you and Nick are sitting in front of him.

The principal says, "I will not allow fighting of any kind in this school. It's my responsibility to make sure that every student is safe on the bus, in the hallways, and in class. Do you understand that everyone has the right to be safe?"

He stops and looks right at you.

"Yes, sir," you answer.

"Yes," Nick answers.

"Well, I want to see just how well you understand the idea of safety," the principal says. "What rules do there need to be to make sure that the bus is a safe place for all students?"

"No fighting, or throwing things," you say.

"No yelling or bothering Mrs. Geller," Nick adds.

Turn to page 54.

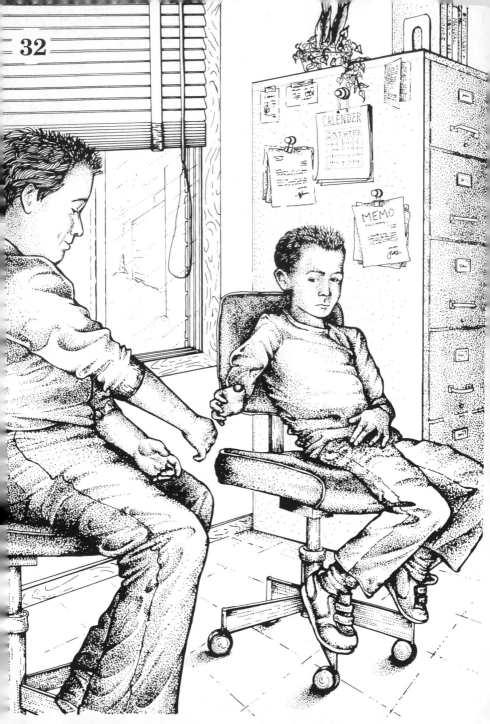

Nick looks over at you and you both just sit there for a long minute. The principal means business, you can tell that very easily.

"Gentlemen, why don't you make it easy on yourselves and forget all this? That way neither of you will get into any more trouble," the principal says.

Finally, you say, "Well, I'm willing to do whatever I have to in order to get this stopped. I just don't want Nick bugging me anymore."

Nick looks over at you again. Then he says, "I don't need any trouble either, let's just forget it."

"Shake," the principal says.

Neither of you want to shake and you are never going to be pals, but it works out okay. A quick shake and it's over.

"I don't want to see you two in the office any more. Do you understand me?"

You both answer "Yes" and walk out of the office.

You weren't too sure that just shaking hands would work—but it did. Nick stopped picking on you for good.

The End

34 You can tell there is no way you and Nick are going to apologize. It is so quiet in the principal's office you can't stand it. He lets you both sit there for a while, hoping that you might change your minds—but it just doesn't happen.

"Okay boys, I'm forced to call your parents."

He calls out to his secretary for your parents' phone numbers and then asks you both to wait outside.

It feels like an awful long time, but then your mom shows up. The principal talks to her alone in his office. A little while later she comes out and says, "Let's go."

When you get in the car she starts talking. "Look Jack, I understand that Nick is picking on you and that you feel you have to do something about it. But fighting is not the answer. The principal can't allow that."

Turn to page 48.

For a while you are both kind of quiet. Then Nick speaks up, "I'd rather do the work during recess than have my parents called."

Both he and the principal look at you. For a minute you think that it really isn't fair. Nick is the bully. You haven't done anything to him. Why should you have to work during recess?

Then you think that maybe it's the easiest way to get this over with. You *could* have the principal call your parents, but that would mean he would call Nick's too. He would be even madder after that and who knows what might happen then?

You say, "Okay, I'll do the work."

"Fine," says the principal, "report here right after lunch. I'll inform your teachers."

For the next month you and Nick do different things around the school during recess. You pick up trash, wash windows, and carry old textbooks to new closets. It isn't all bad. For the first week you don't even talk to Nick, but after a while you do. By the end of the month you even joke about a few things. You're glad when it's over.

The End

It takes you almost a week to decide to stand up **39** to Nick.

You talk it over with your mom and dad. They are helpful, but they keep saying "It's up to you."

Nick keeps bugging you all week. Watching him in the hallway you notice there is one time he is usually alone in his classroom. Just after lunch he always returns a bit early and that is your chance.

One day, standing outside the door, you take a deep breath and walk in.

"Nick, I want to know why you're always bugging me?" you ask.

For a moment he is too surprised to say anything, but then he answers, "I bug you because I like to. Plus, you're so easy. And if you don't leave, I might just do something right now."

"Look, you can beat the heck out of me, but that's no big deal since you weigh about forty pounds more than I do. So if it makes you feel big to beat up on someone smaller, go ahead. It doesn't prove anything. It doesn't make you tough. And it doesn't make you smart."

"Oh, yeah?" says Nick.

"Yeah," you answer, and walk out of the room.

Turn to page 41.

You told your parents what you did. They were proud that you had the nerve to stand up to Nick. You're glad that you never actually had to fight.

The next day on the bus Nick doesn't bother you at all. In fact, *he* ignores *you!* For the first time in a week you feel almost relaxed on the bus.

Later in the day Ben talks to you in the hallway.

"What did you do? Nick didn't say a word to you on the bus," he says.

You smile and say, "Oh, we just had a little talk."

The End

You decide to ask Ms. Wilkins to call Nick in for a meeting between the three of you. You're not sure what she's going to say or do, but you trust her to handle it.

Nick comes in looking like he doesn't know what's going on. He gives you a quick look that sends a chill down your back.

"Nick, Jack," says Ms. Wilkins, "I wanted to have you both in here because I heard there was a problem between you. I understand that you had an argument and now you might fight. I'd like to hear both sides of the story."

Nick looks mad.

"I don't know what lies he's told you, Ms. Wilkins, but—"

"Hey!" you jump in, "I'm not lying about anything, he—"

"Look, boys," Ms. Wilkins interrupts, "we can't straighten it out when you're both this upset. You can calm down now and discuss it, or we can meet later."

If you decide to talk about it now, turn to page 53.

If you decide to meet later, turn to page 45.

Later in the day you meet with Ms. Wilkins and **45** Nick again.

This time you are more calm. You realize that you really want to solve the problem without a fight. Suprisingly, Nick is calmer too.

Pretty soon Ms. Wilkins has you both talking about how you feel. Nick says that you sound like you always know everything and that bothers him. You talk about how you feel on the bus.

"I hope talking about this helps you two to see that the problem can be solved," says Ms. Wilkins. "You don't have to become friends, but you do have to find some way of getting along on the bus and at school."

Nick doesn't quit bugging you right away and he doesn't become a friend, but he does stop picking on you after the talk with Ms. Wilkins.

After a while, Nick doesn't even speak to you anymore.

Another week passes and one day you stop in to see Ms. Wilkins.

"Ms. Wilkins, I just want to say 'thanks.'"

"Thanks for what, Jack?" she asks.

"Just 'thanks,'" you say, and slip out the door.

The End

You decide to tell Mrs. Geller. You pick up your book bag and walk to the front of the bus.

"Jack? What are you doing out of your seat? You know the rule about staying in your seat," she says.

"I know the rule, but there's kind of an emergency back here. Nick is doing all kinds of stuff. He's shooting rubber bands and pencils at me, and calling me names. I just can't take it anymore."

"Nick Jones, get up here right now!" Mrs. Geller yells.

She means business. Nick comes slowly to the front.

"Jack says you're picking on him and shooting things at him. What do you have to say?"

"Me? Mrs. Geller, he's a liar. I don't even talk to him and that's the truth." Nick says, while giving you a look like he wants to eat your nose.

"If you don't agree on what happened, I can't help you. You can work this out in the principal's office," says Mrs. Geller.

Turn to page 25.

48   Your mom keeps talking about the problem. She is pretty honest when she says, "You know, part of me is proud of you for sticking up for yourself. But there are lots of other things you might have tried."

Then you talk about all the different choices you can make when you are having trouble with a bully.

You don't know what happened to Nick that day, whether his parents yelled at him, or what. But you do know the problem stopped once and for all. His parents must have said something to him.

Sometimes you see Nick around school, but he never really bugs you again.

And that is just fine.

The End

50 Mrs. Geller is really mad. She grabs both of you and brings you to the front of the bus. She sends two kids to the back and tells you both to sit down in their seats. The bus suddenly gets very quiet. You and Nick sit without saying a word for the rest of the trip.

When the bus gets to school everyone else gets off first. One kid tries to pat Nick on the back, but Mrs. Geller doesn't let him. Ben winks at you as he passes by.

"Now look," Mrs. Geller says when the bus is empty, "I'm going to give you a choice. I can either take you to the principal right now or I can take you to the office and have your parents come get you."

If you decide you want your mom called, turn to page 29.

If you think Nick is wrong and want to go to the principal, turn to page 31.

You don't know how she did it, but for the next **53** fifteen minutes you are both talking about your worries on the bus and in school.

The strangest thing is that Nick is also talking. He says that he doesn't like the way you sound like you know everything. When you think about that, you realize that he might be right.

Toward the end Ms. Wilkins says, "I'm not trying to make you two friends, but I am trying to settle this problem. If there is a fight, you won't be thinking about your school work, and you will end up in the principal's office. I don't think you'd like that.

"One way for people to settle an argument is to let them talk it out. We've had a chance to do that, but it doesn't end here. Now you have to make some decisions. You can either stay angry at each other or you can stop it. I hope you think a lot about it."

You are still kind of mad. Nick doesn't look too happy either. Ms. Wilkins looks at both of you.

"Maybe we need to talk about this some more," she suggests. "I'd like both of you to come see me after school today."

Turn to page 45.

"I want you two to solve this problem," says the principal. "I see four different ideas. You boys can choose any one.

"First, you can shake hands, promise to stop all this arguing and go your separate ways.

"Second, if you refuse to apologize, then I can call your parents. They can take you home and deal with you.

"Third, if you don't want to apologize, and don't want your parents called in, I'll simply let them know that I'm taking care of the problem. You will both have to work around the school during recess for a month.

"Last, we talked a lot about safety. The rules you boys came up with are the ones you have to follow so that everyone on the bus is safe. If you think you can do that, I want you to come back here in three days and we'll see how it is working out."

"What'll it be?" he asks, looking straight at you.

If you decide to apologize, turn to page 33.

If you decide to let the principal call your parents, turn to page 34.

If you decide to do the work at school, turn to page 36.

If you decide to act safely on the bus, turn to page 56.

About ten or twelve boys walk up to where Nick
is standing with his friends near the bus. He looks
around and says, "What's this? The teacher's pet
patrol?"

Ben steps forward. He looks a little scared.
"Nick, all of us want you to stop picking on Jack.
You're bothering him for no good reason. Maybe
you're doing it just because you're bigger than he
is."

"That's right. Leave him alone!" the other boys
join in.

"Who's going to stop me?" Nick asks.

Neither you nor Ben are sure that this was the
right thing to do. You stand in the back of the
crowd. Then you hear one of the fifth graders
speak up.

"You heard Ben. All of us are going to stop you,"
he says.

At first Nick looks like he's going to laugh, then
he looks unsure. Finally, he turns and walks away
with his friends.

Since then, Nick hasn't spoken to you again.
And you gained a bunch of new friends.

The End

56   After meeting with the principal earlier in the day, you are worried about riding on the bus. You figure that walking home or getting a ride would make you a chicken, so you head for the bus.

Nick is standing right by the door. You take a big breath and walk by him. Your shoulder brushes against his. He gives you a dirty look, but doesn't say anything. You hurry to get on the bus.

For the next three days that's the way it goes. Nick looks at you funny, but he never says or does anything.

Turn to page 58.

Ben runs around the corner of the school where he knows some friends always hang out in the morning. Most of the boys are in the fourth grade, but there are a few fifth graders too.

Ben tells them about the problem you are having with Nick. Not too many fourth and fifth graders like Nick. Ben asks if they will help stop the fight. He doesn't want them to make it worse, just to help stop it.

For a while, it is quiet while the boys think it over.

A fifth grader says, "Hey, if we all go and stick together, Nick will *have* to listen."

A few others nod their heads. One boy says, "Let's go have a talk with Nick."

Turn to page 55

Three days pass and you and Nick are again in the principal's office. He looks at both of you closely. Finally, he smiles.

"Well, gentlemen, I guess you understand a little about responsibility now. Everyone has to be able to come to school without worrying about getting picked on. Everyone has the right to feel safe. I'm proud of you, and I hope this problem is solved."

You and Nick don't become friends, but you don't have any more problems either.

The End